KEN RANEY

IT'S PROBABLY GOOD
DINOSAURS
ARE EXTINCT

*To Chase.
Ken Raney
11-18-93*

GREEN TIGER PRESS
PUBLISHED BY SIMON & SCHUSTER
NEW YORK   LONDON   TORONTO   SYDNEY   TOKYO   SINGAPORE

I love dinosaurs. In fact, I love dinosaurs so much that I have always thought I'd like to have one for a pet. But when I really think about it—it's probably good that dinosaurs are extinct.

Just imagine how different the world would be if dinosaurs were alive today. Think how big the zoo would have to be.

A drive in the country would come to a sudden (and long) halt if a herd of apatosaurus wanted to cross the road.

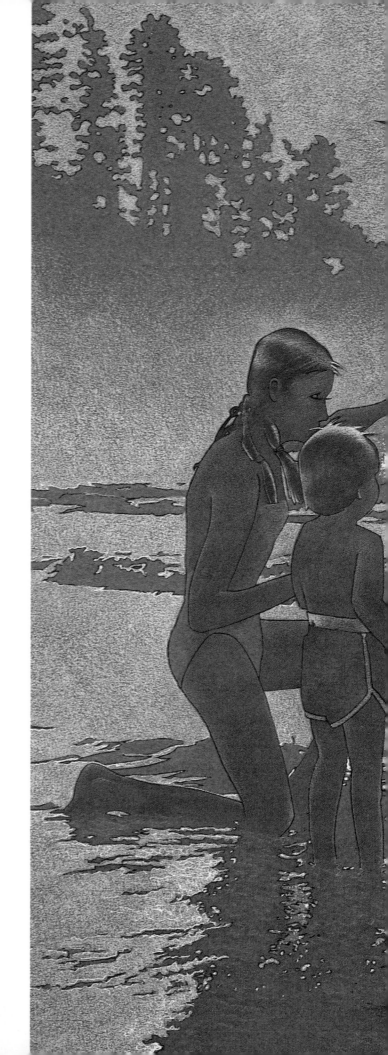

And there would be more than dolphins and sea gulls to watch on a trip to the beach.

The world's most famous places would certainly look different if dinosaurs still roamed the earth. There might be pterosaurs at the pyramids.

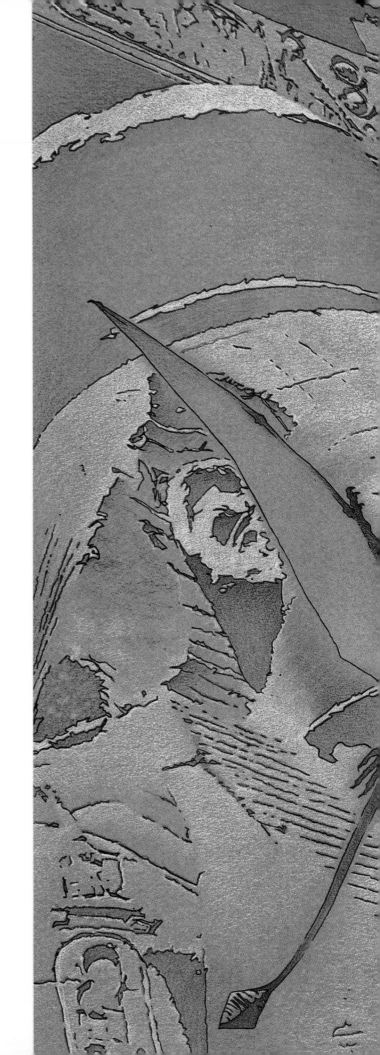

And at Redwood National Forest, the brachiosaurs would be nearly as tall as the trees.

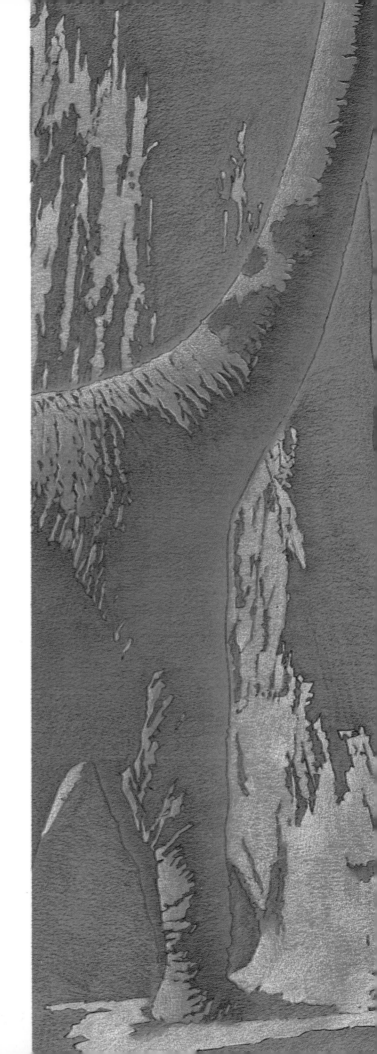

History would be very different if dinosaurs had not become extinct. It certainly would have taken Noah a lot longer to build the ark if he'd had to make room for two of every dinosaur.

And what a sight it would have been to see a stegosaurus hitched to a covered wagon in the Old West.

C an you imagine how difficult some jobs would be if dinosaurs still existed? It would take real courage to be a paperboy.

And a rodeo cowboy
wouldn't want to get
bucked off a protoceratops!

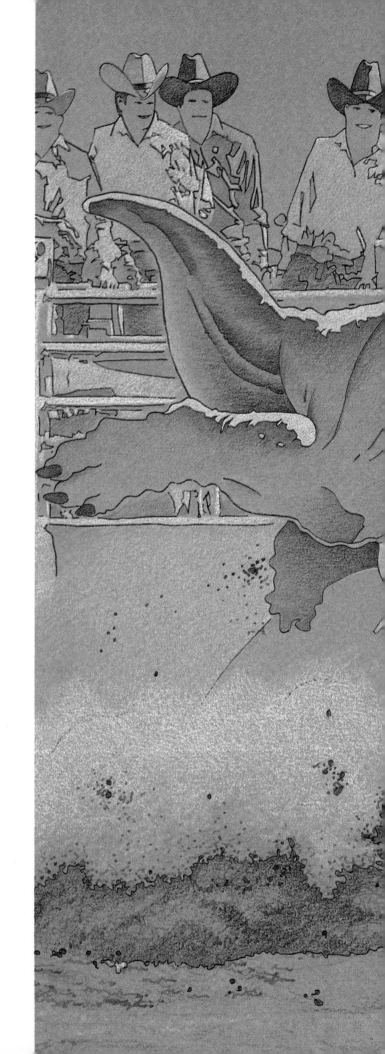

And can you imagine
what it would be like to be
a veterinarian?

Still, dinosaurs could be very useful for some things. In a parade, apatosaurus would always attract a crowd.

And wouldn't a struthiomimus look grand in the winner's circle at the Kentucky Derby?

But, most of all,
if dinosaurs were still
around, think how much
moms and dads would
dread hearing:
"Can I keep him . . . please?"

So I guess, all in all, it's probably good that dinosaurs are extinct.

"In the beginning,
God created the heavens
and the earth."
GENESIS 1:1

To Mom & Dad

K.R.

GREEN TIGER PRESS
Simon & Schuster Building, Rockefeller Center
1230 Avenue of the Americas, New York, New York 10020
Copyright © 1993 by Ken Raney
GREEN TIGER PRESS is an imprint of Simon & Schuster.
Designed by Sylvia Frezzolini.
Manufactured in the United States of America

10 9 8 7 6 5 4 3 2 1

Library of Congress Cataloging-in-Publication Data
Raney, Ken. It's probably good dinosaurs are
extinct / by Ken Raney. p. cm. Summary: A boy
imagines how different things would be if dinosaurs
still roamed the earth. [1. Dinosaurs—Fiction.]
PZ7.R162It 1993 92-33739
[E]—dc20   CIP   AC
ISBN: 0-671-86576-5